Fancy NANCY
and the Late, Late, LATE Night

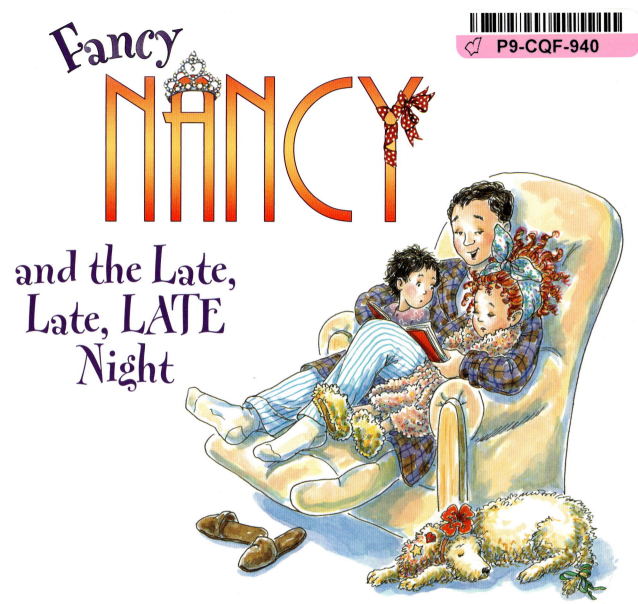

Based on *Fancy Nancy* written by Jane O'Connor

Cover illustration by Robin Preiss Glasser

Interior illustrations by Carolyn Bracken

HARPER FESTIVAL

An Imprint of HarperCollinsPublishers

HarperFestival is an imprint of HarperCollins Publishers.

Fancy Nancy and the Late, Late, LATE Night
Text copyright © 2010 by Jane O'Connor
Illustrations copyright © 2010 by Robin Preiss Glasser
www.harpercollinschildrens.com
Library of Congress catalog card number: 2009942167
ISBN 978-0-06-170377-5

Book design by Sean Boggs
13 SCP 20 19 18 17 16 15 14 13
❖
First Edition

I adore visiting my neighbor Mrs. DeVine.
Here we are having tea on her veranda.
(That's a fancy word for porch.)

When she was a child, Mrs. DeVine lived in Hollywood. She used to see lots of movie stars—only Mrs. DeVine calls them celebrities.
Isn't that fancy?

She has a special scrapbook of photographs.
Some are autographed.
That means celebrities signed them.

"Your scrapbook is extremely fascinating," I say.
(Fascinating is even more interesting than interesting.)

Ooh la la! Mrs. DeVine says I can borrow her scrapbook if I bring it back tomorrow. "Merci, merci, merci!" I say.

At home I pretend that I am a Hollywood celebrity.
I dress up in my most glamorous attire—that's fancy for clothes.

I give my autograph to all my fans.

I pose for photographs.

"I am late for a glamorous Hollywood party," I tell my fans.
"Au revoir!"
(You say it like this: aw ruh-VWA. That's French for "good-bye.")

On my door I put up a sign that says
Do Not Disturb,
because celebrities need their privacy.
I want to look through Mrs. DeVine's scrapbook,
but I hear my dad calling us all to dinner.

After dinner I learn all my spelling words.
I am practically an expert at spelling.
Before I know it, Mom says, "Nancy, time for bed."
Oh no! I haven't had a second to look at the scrapbook.

I beg my mom to let me stay up later. But my mom says no.
"It's a school night. Tomorrow is Friday.
Tomorrow you can stay up later."

I put on my nightie and get in bed.

My parents kiss me good night.
"Sleep tight," they say.

But guess what! I am not going to sleep.
Under the covers, I have concealed—
that's fancy for hidden—
a flashlight and the scrapbook.

I stay up very late.
It is almost ten o'clock when I put away the scrapbook
and turn off my flashlight.
I bet even celebrities don't stay up this late!

The next morning, when my dad wakes me up,
I am exhausted. Exhausted is even worse than tired.

At recess, I am too exhausted to jump rope with Bree and my friends.

I miss three of the words on the spelling list.
My brain is exhausted, too.

After school, I return Mrs. DeVine's scrapbook.
She asks if I would like to stay for dinner
and watch a movie called *National Velvet*.

"It is on TV tonight. It is about a girl and a horse.
I loved it when I was your age," she says.
It sounds fascinating, but I can hardly keep my eyes open.

I go home and start weeping—which is fancy for crying.
When my dad asks what's wrong, I confess.
"I was naughty. I stayed up late last night and
I had a terrible and exhausting day."

My dad doesn't scold me. He says, "Now you understand why you need a good night's sleep."

That night I go to bed even earlier than my sister!

On Saturday I wake up feeling glorious again.
(Glorious is fancy for wonderful.)

And guess what—Mrs. DeVine taped the movie for me!
I can see it tonight.
Dad was right—even fancy girls need their beauty rest.